Pip Likes Snow

First published 2005
Evans Brothers Limited
2A Portman Mansions
Chiltern Street
London W1U 6NR

British Library Cataloguing in Publication Data
Rickards, Lynne
        Pip likes snow. - (Twisters)
        1. Children's stories - Pictorial works
        I. Title
        823.9'2 [J]

ISBN-10: 0237530759
13-digit ISBN (from 1 January 2007) 9780237530754

Printed in China by Wing King Tong Co. Ltd

Series Editor: Nick Turpin
Design: Robert Walster
Production: Jenny Mulvanny
Series Consultant: Gill Matthews

Pip Likes Snow

Lynne Rickards
and Belinda Worsley

Pip lives at the South Pole.

Pip likes snow.

He can slide.

Pip likes ice.

He can skate.

Pip likes water.

15

He can dive.

He can swim.

He can catch fish.

21

Pip has lots of friends.

He likes a party!

He makes a wish.

Most of all, Pip loves...

29

holidays!

Why not try reading another Twisters book?